COMMON THREADZ

COMMON THREADZ

(THE LOGIC OF ENLIGHTENMENT)

Written by:

"You"

Copyright © 2021 by You.

All rights reserved. No part of this book may be reproduced in any form or by any electronic or mechanical means, including information storage and retrieval systems, without permission in writing from the publisher, except by reviewers, who may quote brief passages in a review.

ISBN: 978-1-956736-58-8 (Paperback Edition)
ISBN: 978-1-956736-59-5 (Hardcover Edition)
ISBN: 978-1-956736-57-1 (E-book Edition)

Some characters and events in this book are fictitious. Any similarity to the real persons, living or dead, is coincidental and not intended by the author.

Book Ordering Information

Phone Number: 315 288-7939 ext. 1000 or 347-901-4920
Email: info@globalsummithouse.com
Global Summit House
www.globalsummithouse.com

Printed in the United States of America

FOREWORD...

Enlightenment has been a mysterious and elusive treasure that I've passionately searched for all my life. I have looked everywhere that was told to have insight or instruction. I have studied the nature of life and existence on our planet from every perspective or angle that I can find. This book is an objective intellectual summary of all that I've learned, along with some profound discoveries. I now have the wonderful good fortune of having found a perspective that brings me complete peace. One that allows me to go through life without being bothered by the past, present, or future. I love every living creature, and the story and relationship we all share. I have faith for the human race and our future because I've seen glimpses of the amazing capability of team effort. Let's be very clear, we are part of team human and we are currently failing as a team...

    We live in a society that is changing faster than most of us can keep track of. Throughout this book you will gain a withdrawn perspective on all that is happening around us in this changing world. I will discuss some of the painful truths of our reality, and the unfortunate condition we find ourselves in. I will give light to the cause of the epidemic of anxiety and depression that you likely see around you, and quite possibly in your own life. I will help pinpoint some of the things that cause us this unidentifiable but constant discomfort, and provide an explanation and solution to them.

This book will provide a simple and streamline perspective from which you can view your own life in this intellectually demanding time in history. I offer a spiritual and intellectual common ground for mankind that can bridge gaps between faiths, between theories, between nations, between neighbors. I will provide a step-by-step thought process to help alleviate and even eliminate the cumbersome emotional baggage that you may be carrying, and offer a direct path to attaining and finding your own enlightenment.

I encourage everyone to explore and learn truths for themselves. Research facts and draw your own conclusions about the world you live in. While knowledge can uncover some ugly truths, if you keep at it there is profound insight and a sustainable faith to be gathered.

THE CONDITION...

It can be so difficult to try and find our own well-being in this modern society. For most of us, society generally feels like a convoluted judgemental mess. Participating creates complex confusion in ourselves and seems to breed anxiety, insecurity, and ultimately depression. Those that even care to look for spiritual answers find convincing contradicting arguments for any topic they can possibly seek. Thousands of different religions and ways of thought that seem to be bickering over supremacy. Unfortunately, our world has changed from a society of faith to a society of facts because of this discord. So many aspects of the many different religious histories or folklores have been scientifically disproven now as well. Many people that follow a religion these days resort to not taking the doctrine verbatim, and they try and just sift through to find their own meaning. The younger generation that's growing up being able to instantly fact check just aren't buying it…

    I recall being disappointed and disheartened myself when I realized there was still no spiritual common ground to speak of amongst humanity. I set out inspired and excited to find something higher to believe in whole-heartedly… and ended up seeking my own truth because of a lack of solidarity. It seemed in order to follow a religion and believe, I would need to ignore the others and have faith that they were either mistaken or misguided. I actually lost a bit of faith in our intelligence and evolution as a species, knowing that after all this time we still couldn't agree on the most fundamental aspect of life as a human. Whether we are Gods or are made by them/him/her/it. Whether to forgive or seek revenge. Whether we evolved or were created. Whether the universe was created for us or if we were insignificant. We can't even agree on whether to be kind to our neighbors! Though obviously, it's not generally practiced..

After a duration of seeking a spiritual explanation of the reality in which we live, with no avail, I then turned to science to at least learn the nature of things on an elemental and functional level. I was again surprised to learn that at the basis of things, we operate under several different quantum theories that as you might guess, completely contradict each other. It seems that most of them offer a great explanation of certain aspects of our reality, but none of them offer a complete explanation that is applicable to all that we know of our physical world. I lost a bit of faith again when I realized that we sidestepped finding a universal truth, so we could continue our advancement. Generally speaking, our entire scientific basis of understanding on this planet is based on assumptions that were "close enough."

For example, The widely accepted Big Bang Theory is based on the fact that we noticed the universe itself seems to be expanding. Operating on this assumption, we decided that everything that exists used to be in one big ball that exploded one day. We go farther to assume where that ball originally existed, and by the distance of the farthest stars that we can see, we have also decided on a birth date of the universe and when the explosion happened. This trail of assumptions is factored into equations and theories all over the globe… however, it isn't verified in what we see taking place out there. If it was, planets and galaxies would be slowly coming to a halt. What we actually found in time, is that the universe's expansion is in fact speeding up instead of slowing down. This doesn't stand to reason with what we know of physics…

So the idea of dark matter was born. The notion that the expanse of space has something else in it that is pulling on our physical universe as a cumulative. Logically speaking, the increasing speed of the expansion of our universe should in fact discredit The Big Bang Theory. However, we did not discard it, we merely created another theory to stack on top of it. Ironically, in order for an individual to believe wholeheartedly in this science, you just have to have "faith" in the idea…

The intellectual mind is a curious thing. We like to believe that we know for certain what's going on around us. When facts or situations arise that seem to disprove what we believe, we turn a blind eye to them and try and move forward with our fingers jammed tightly into our ears, metaphorically. This method of securing our understanding of things has worked well for thousands of years. However, in the 21st century our intellects have reached a point that we are bothered by assumptions and gaps in our perceptions. We want answers. We want a belief system that satisfies our need to know for sure. The obstacle that we face in that pursuit is that in order to find a universal truth, all parties involved would have to agree that we are wrong. So the period of time from when we threw our hands up to say that we were ignorant, to the time where we finally put the pieces together in a correct way, can be ominous. Being in an intellectual limbo without an answer is unnerving to say the least.

The growing social trend now is a general disgust for the way civilization is being managed. For the manner that our resources are gathered, handled, and spent. For the blatant manipulation of the masses. For the obvious greed that pulls the strings and shapes our lives. For the overall misguidance we receive on what foods are healthy. For the general disregard for our planet and future generations… People are fed up, and to an intellectually graduated mass of people like ourselves, our leaders look like self-entitled medieval dictators and are taking us for complete idiots. People outwardly don't care because we feel individually helpless against the aspects of our society that disgust us. People claim to have "no fucks to give" and "you only live once, so who cares?" Having our entire history available online shows us the that we shouldn't openly trust anything we're told, as we have been played for fools and sent to war time and again over the disagreements of the wealthy and entitled. It's clear that each of us is considered to be an expendable resource by our leaders. That's terribly harming to an intellect. And doesn't cultivate a sense of community.

Our society and reality has changed greatly in recent years. It seems that most of our lives are now guided and governed by a virtual wellspring of information. If you don't have a good online presence you probably don't have many friends in real life. We are the first generation of our species that is wrestling with more of an intellectual and emotional challenge then our physical one. We don't need to move boulders with our hands anymore, we find a piece of equipment that we can use to do the job. We don't need to memorize books, appointments, or any info that can instantly be referenced because of its availability through our electronic devices. We don't even need a sense of direction anymore, as the paths are already laid out for us, and your device will check with the satellites and to tell you which route is fastest. We drive, float, and fly across the landscape on roads and in vehicles that were created by the sweat and struggle of our forefathers. They worked their entire lives to provide an easier life for us than they had to endure… and succeeded.

We in fact enjoy a much easier and more comfortable existence then any of our ancestors have. However, in this technologically advanced world we live in, we are forging new ground in the evolution of the human mind as we speak. There has never been a time in history where man had to struggle with the duality of an online presence as well as their own physical image. While we may now have a much faster mental processing speed, and a multi-faceted sense of reality, we have far less capacity for things like patience, memory, and quite apparently reverence. We have virtually any form of entertainment or stimulation at our fingertips at any time of the day. Whatever your current mood or whim is, you can find a week's worth of that exact entertainment or interaction. What this creates is a complete lack of patience or excitement for every day things. You don't have to wait for anything anymore. You can most likely eat, watch, play, or read anything you can think of tonight, and you know that. So life becomes unimpressive. Your own life (in comparison to all the entertainment you can see right now) is most likely boring and ultimately unsatisfying.

We spend so much time in our virtual world, that we are losing our talents to interact in our physical one. Everywhere you go you see people in crowds and groups who are not interacting with each other. Everyone is looking down at their devices, and not paying attention to the people that are next to them. Real-life, real-time conversation is diminishing along with eye contact, and many types of interaction. Ironically, we are in the most crowded and overpopulated state that we have ever been in history. Yet we have social anxiety because we would rather turn our attention to our devices. This general disconnection between people applies to intimate or sexual engagement as well. Many people look to their devices for intimate or sexual stimulation now. They spend so much time being able to pick whatever they're in the mood for, that in real life situations they are less interested or engaged in the moment. For many this overstimulation effects their performance and even success. If this trend continues or even intensifies I would suspect it will act as a inevitable population control administered by fate.

Every creature in existence has to struggle to survive, propagate, or have dominance. This has been the story of mankind as well since it began. Comparison and competition ensure that the strong or successful survive. So despite a relatively comfortable existence where most of us don't need to fight or kill for our next meal, we find ourselves constantly struggling and fighting with each other instead. Mostly, fighting to protect our image or reputation. We have to understand that the desire to struggle and fight is hardwired into our brains. When something is wrong we feel like we need to fight or argue about it. We love drama! If there isn't anything dramatic happening, we'll create some! This is why dramatic entertainment reigns supreme in ratings, always. But if we are to advance as individuals or as a civilization, we need to calm our inner warrior and start to learn how to communicate productively.

Our Instinct as humans is to try and fit in with whatever group we are surrounded by. This has always been our genetically programmed directive. Fitting in and following suit ensures we are not left alone or without. We try to blend in and model ourselves after the most successful or common of our predecessors. This is the preprogrammed function of most all life. But the process of evolution lies in the variations that inevitably surface over time. At a certain point the adaptation that is better suited becomes the dominant habit of that species, and in turn a permanent behavioral modification follows. As humans, similarly, when we are proficient at what normal behavior requires, then we have time to analyze what the masses are doing, and sometimes find a new outlook or adaptation that is more logical or productive. We then have to ask ourselves if our effort is better spent trying to yell loud enough to get the masses to change, or if it is better to just become the embodiment of what that solution is. If you feel that people should be more patient, considerate, and compassionate, then that should be exactly what you would embody in your day. Others see your behavior and recognize its merit, and they start to take example. If we can reach a point where we are the majority opinion in any situation then naturally the masses will follow suit... Without a battle or argument having to take place, a resolve is achieved on a grand scale.

Finding and applying solutions is a difficult process in a society as developed as our own. Before change can be made, the majority of the masses need to be convinced that change is even necessary. At a glance, that seems like it would be an obvious need in today's convoluted society, but people hold tightly to their habits, and hate admitting they're wrong. In a time like this, he who controls the advertising controls the masses. Our Individual voices are too small to be heard above the rush of media, and we recognize their insignificance, so most often we choose to just give up trying to educate others and become slighted at what "normal" is. Spiritually, we will likely wear that feeling throughout our lives. Believe it or not, most everyone you meet share that same disheartened feeling. It is clearly necessary for all of our singular voices to become unified in some way. This would magnify our intentions to a point that they would have to be heard with reverence. Herein lies the problem. We are all over the board with our opinions. In order to progress we have to admit that we were wrong, and be open to change.

When 1,000 people take a guess at the number of pebbles in a jar, most likely none of them will give the correct answer. But when you compile their answers and create an average, the sum will likely be very close to exact. This is called crowd wisdom and applies to all things. We may not singularly have the correct answer but we most certainly have the cumulative one. In any setting or situation, a group of people is most successful and productive when they work together as a team. Discord and conflict amongst any team will harm that groups success. We live in a place with limited resources, limited time, and limited energy. As we forge our way into the 21st century we need to be doing so in an effective and efficient manner. The billions of individuals involved in mankind have a limitless capability to achieve things, if we are united. If we continue to try and find universal understandings while we are bickering and fighting with one another, we will be wasting a large portion of our energy, and will inevitably fall short.

The time is now to established some form of universal truth to all things. Close to 1 million humans will commit suicide this year on the planet Earth. This means that the general condition of society is such that a million citizens would rather give up their lives then participate in this judgemental and combative game we've created to occupy ourselves. 75% of young adults from the age of 12 to 22 are clinically depressed and virtually on the verge of suicide. In a recent poll, it was found that 60% of American college students would rather die then spend 8 hours alone with their thoughts in a room with nothing but a chair. There's a huge amount of homeless adolescents today that simply don't want to participate in this society, and would much rather live on the street. THERE IS A HUGE PROBLEM IN THIS! The condition of the human experience is facing a paradigm shift. The leaders that orchestrate and control our lives are not going to make effort to establish peace amongst the population. Quite simply, a unified population of people is scary to a system that is trying to control or manipulate them.

The result of this wellspring of debate among mankind is obvious. When we pass by strangers out on the world we look at each other sideways, wondering what each other believe or stand for. Wondering what side each other support. Assuming that others believe differently than us, and disregarding the kindness or respect that's given, because it is likely done with an ulterior motive. We judge others at a glance by skin color, fashion sense, dialect, music taste, vehicle choice, house, neighborhood, state, hats, hairstyle, shoes, etc. We lack a general respect and sense of community in our cities and as nations. We feel justified in our doubt for others intentions because we only feel that we need to support our "side". But let's be very clear, happening across someone who shares your style, musical taste, religious views, political views, social views, and moral standpoint on the various topics of debate is like looking for a unicorn. We alienate ourselves with our judgements and are simultaneously feeling lonely. We are good people with good intentions, who are frustrated and giving up trying to make a difference. Its difficult to have faith in people's words, and motives… but we desperately want to! We are the generation that needs to make change for the sake of mankind.

Now let's learn how to logically do so…

THE MEASURE OF SELF...

Imagine yourself standing in front of an enormous libra scale with a brass bowl on either side. On one side small black pebbles are collected, and on the other side small gold coins are collected. Imagine the scale as a representation of the story of your life. Each gold coin represents a good deed or kindness that you've done. Each time you share kindness with someone, they walk away feeling a little brighter, lighter, or more forgiving. They, in turn, will share the positive feeling you left with them with someone else. You as well get a coin for the good deed that that person shared your kindness with, and so on. As you might imagine, they add up quickly. On the other side of the scale, each black pebble represents a rude gesture, a put down, a blind eye to someone in need. Just as with your good deeds, when you pass on negativity to someone they walk away feeling irritated, short, combative, or disheartened. They will pass that negative feeling you gave to them onto someone else, and you receive another black pebble, and so on.

You see, we inadvertently send waves of disposition and intention throughout our neighborhood, city, and corner of the world. You've seen this exchange manifested in many ways. It takes only a few minutes for someone in a terrible mood to spoil a room full of people who were previously enjoying themselves. This is as well true for someone who's having the best time of their lives in a room full of people that are down. If you've been in a poor mood for a time, you should expect to experience that similar mood from others. If you've been in a great mood, you will likely run across more people who are in a similar great mood. It's quite possible in either situation that you are experiencing people who have indirectly been affected by the mood that you put out onto others. This is most noticeable in a workplace or family situation where you are exposed to particular individuals frequently over time.

For instance… you are the manager at your workplace and are having an off-day. A supervisor beneath you comes into your office and says something that makes you feel insecure about your worth. You make a rude comment to him or her and they go back about their workday feeling unappreciated. Throughout the day they project that feeling to all of their employees. You notice by the end of the day that several employees have made rude remarks to one another, or even to you. Because of your current mood, you decide to punish them and words are exchanged. That evening, unknowingly, you and all of your employees sit at your homes and lament about your day. Most likely some of your families received a portion of the bad mood you came home with as well. All of you feel unappreciated, and are not enthusiastic about going to work the following day. Though each of you may feel completely justified in how you acted or reacted in that situation, you are all at fault. Your emotionally wounded perspective allowed you to be harmed by someone's harmless comment, and you decided to retaliate. Naturally, everyone else in the workplace followed suit. In this situation you find a large group of people who will now be on guard, combative, and uncooperative. Inevitably, the productivity of that day was harmed due to the discord of the parties involved. The business may have even made less money that day. Everyone ended up paying a price, though none of you feel responsible.

We tend to operate under the general assumption that most of the insignificant things we do in our day don't matter. That our choices in those situations are inconsequential. This isn't at all true, and later we'll find out to what extent. These small choices tend to collect on our spirit whether we admit it or ever share it with anyone. Thinking back over your life you can imagine what type of balance of pebbles and coins you may have accumulated. This general sense of your own balance effectively describes your well-being . Most people are probably divided somewhere around 60/40 toward one side or another. This measure can give you a visual reference about how you likely feel about yourself. Unfortunately, as much as you might be convinced that you do a good job of hiding how you really feel from the people around you, you radiate that feeling and they end up wearing it as well, to an extent. If you regularly share company with someone they likely have a better idea of how you feel about yourself then you do. It seems to be relatively impossible to actually hide your feelings for any length of time from those that are close to you. This is exponentially true for your mate. If you sleep next to someone on a daily basis and you are feeling terrible, they will likely have a hard time trying to feel good in themselves. When people are close to us in an emotional way, we automatically feel a certain responsibility for their mood, whether it has anything to do with us or not. For those who are aware, it's clear to see that all of our words, responses, and interactions are filtered through what mood we're in. There is a certain processing that goes on in your mind as you choose what words to build your sentences with, that regards your personality and disposition towards the topic at hand. Certain particular responses tend to become a habit, and ingrain themselves in your personality or image. In a sense, we practice our usual disposition like a martial art. We don't change overnight, and finding a certain balance with things can take a years of practice. We don't get to snap our fingers and have peace, usually. Though after spending a few months, years, or decades practicing it, it will become second nature.

Sometimes a person's positive gold coins outweigh their negative pebbles to such an extent that they can reach up and grab one of the coins. Meaning they had practiced that positive sentiment so often that they truly understand the coins value, and can hand out insight or intention directly. Of course, as you hand them out, more coins fall in their place… this applies to the black pebbles of your negative sentiments as well. After a certain time of practice, one can master these positive or negative sentiments, and project them so often that they find themselves swimming in either gold coins or black pebbles. Most all of us do both good and bad things. We spread positivity when we feel good. We reflect negativity when we feel upset. When thinking of your life from the perspective of balance, it's clear to see that it is really never too late to start tipping your scales in a more productive way. Some of the most wonderful things that have been done in history were done so by people who were trying to redeem themselves.

Quite simply, if you want to feel good… be nice. If you maneuver your life in such a way where you have no regret or guilt for the choices you've made, then people's opinions of you become irrelevant. With some practice you can quickly achieve a feeling of confidence that can't be taken from you. In fact, you reach a point where there are no sore subjects for you, you are open minded, accepting, and not able to be offended.

How you feel affects how you carry yourself. How you carry yourself affects the influence you have on others. The influence you have on others affects how they interact or cooperate with you. How people interact with you affects your self-esteem. Of course, your self esteem affects how successful you are at any given task or endeavor, and ultimately how you feel about yourself. Your intentions in this world affect every morsel of your experience in this life…

THE POWER OF INTENTION

Most of what we know about our daily life and existence revolves around what we physically do and identify as. While these things are relevant, they really only regard half of the experience we are having here as human beings. When seeking enlightenment it's important to first understand what and how your energy works. The fact that we have a spiritual energy aside from our physical body is universally accepted around the world, for the most part. Most religions and even some avenues of science will agree that we are spiritual beings that inhabit physical bodies, and when your life ceases your spirit continues. There are six main aspects of our spiritual existence that have been proven in clinical studies and accepted scientifically. Telekinesis (manipulating matter), telepathy (reading minds or intentions), remote viewing (being able to envision things outside your experience), power of prayer (group intentions having a physical effect on health), cumulative consciousness (a telepathic interconnection in large groups of life forms), and of course, communication with spirit (being able to spiritually connect with those who have passed.) It is said that while some people have automatic talents in any of these areas, everyone has intuition and capability of some form or another. Government agencies around the world have been using people with specific extra-sensory abilities for decades.

Energy is in everything around us. Your whole existence is

surrounded by, fed by, and carried out by your energy. Your brain is a symphony of tiny lightning bolts operating on a harmonic frequency that is specifically yours. Everything that you've experienced and know thus far is stored in your brain on small bits of energy called neurons. Approximately 84 billion neurons are in the average brain. Each one has neuro pathways to 1000 others, and fire as often as 200 times per second. Every movement, intuition, feeling, and emotion is a small bolt of energy being transferred around your body. Hundreds or even thousands of them every second. Scientifically speaking, when someone is staring at you and you can feel it, they are shooting a small stream of encoded energy from their mind to your body. The part of your body that's receiving that signal informs your mind, and your mind tries to decipher who it is, and what it is that's staring at you. Danger is immediately evaluated, and your mind goes further to read specific intentions. If someone is looking at a part of your body, you can feel it tingle physically so you cover it or display it. If someone is staring at you that loves you, that feels very different than someone staring at you that hates you. It usually only takes a few seconds of staring at someone in a busy crowded place before they will decipher the signal and look directly at you. If you pick an obscure part of someone's body and stare at it in a quiet setting, a few seconds later they will itch that spot unknowingly. Usually, your direct attention is noticed almost instantly but after a period of about 3 seconds a connection starts to develop, and you start to exchange intention back and forth. This is why you will often find people start to get uncomfortable if you look at them longer than just a brief glance. Realistically, most of our exchange and interaction back and forth with other people in your life is not verbal. We read each other's sentiments and intentions all day long, every single day. I call this interaction the "Constant Telepathic Exchange".

Most of you have probably noticed the common coincidence that when someone crosses your mind, even from across the globe, they will contact you. Or perhaps you've noticed that you are bothered by the feeling that people are talking bad about you. Maybe you've noticed how it can be uncanny that when you change your emotional sentiments towards someone, the next time you see them your sentiment was reciprocated before you reunited. Or when something traumatic happens to a loved one or family member, and you suddenly get an uneasy feeling in your stomach. 200 years ago, (before instant communication,) when a loved one passed you felt it and set off on the journey to their home, and as you arrived you would find that other family members or loved ones were as well arriving at the same time. Once you are closely acquainted to someone your mind is aware of their specific harmonic frequency, and you associate that frequency with the memory of that person. When something physically or emotionally changes in that person's life, you almost instantaneously receive an intuitive message. It's like your mind knows the specific address of someone else's spirit and can decipher and differentiate it from the barrage of different intentions that are circling about. Exactly like two cell phones communicating through a satellite that carries thousands of other signals, but only receiving each other's.

Your mind processes thousands of bits of information about your surroundings every second. Your conscious mind is only aware of a handful of those. This is because our conscious mind only consists of the matters of our interaction, well-being, and survival. Once you accept intuition as being real, your perception of reality changes. Most of the time that we come across these uncanny coincidences we discredit them as merely being ironic or odd. In actuality, we are just for a moment noticing the Constant Telepathic Exchange we are usually obliviously taking part in. Whether we take note or not, you are exchanging telepathic information with everyone from a random person at the grocery store, to the guy that cut you off in traffic this morning, to your closest friends, and as well your enemies. Whoever you are , smart or not, you can feel each others hidden directives or emotions, and your mind quite possibly is communicating your thoughts and intentions with someone this very moment.

When you are at the market and you make eye contact with someone across the room, you can feel if this person just thought "what's this lady looking at!?" As you approach, you will likely wear a combative or resentful sentiment. They glance at you again, see your disposition clearly, and react accordingly. Most likely you at least exchange a disapproving look, if not words as well. You both walk away wondering what the others problem with you was, not realizing that you may have inadvertently sparked that exchange. Basically if you walk around the world in a poor and combative mood, don't be surprised if the people you encounter are equally combative towards you. Even when you haven't yet spoken to them. When you look to see if someone has called, right as they're calling. When someone is humming the song that you just had in your head. When a church full of people pray for someone's health and they suddenly get better. When large groups of people meditate in the effort of peace in a large city, the crime rate goes down considerably for the following week. There is in fact repeated concrete evidence of global synchronicities in nature during times where humanity has a common focus. During New Year's every year and even events such as the 9/11 attack, synchronicities in electronic probability monitoring devices are shown from several hours before to several hours after these events. The devices are placed around the world, generate numbers randomly, and keep record of the sequence. During these events of cumulative intention the devices produce the exact same numbers in the exact same sequences. The probability of this happening randomly is virtually impossible. These events where mankind is singularly focused on anything at all actually affect these electronic devices. It's as though we create an instant of global well being.

We very much are individual beings that share a collective

consciousness. Our actions are felt in a small way through the whole population. These aren't just inspirational words to put on a poster, this is the fundamental reality that we live in. When I start my day and head out into the world, I'm counting on you and everyone you know, in order to have a good day. As you may be already aware, you can start your day in a great mood and by the time you've interacted with 10 people on your way to work, you can be in a terrible mood… and of course spread it to everyone else you see that day. We quite literally are depending on each other in order to be enjoying this life and this civilization together. There's a term called Heliotropic Management. It refers to the practice of being considerate and kind when you are in a position of control over people. You make it a point to learn people's names, things about there lives, and you show interest in them as people. Through the natural order of things, those employees then feel better about the job they are doing, work harder, show more teamwork, and are likely to defend their coworkers and the company as a whole because of that positive representation. Profits increase, productivity increases, and job retention as well, obviously. The entire functionality of that business or its endeavors run better when employees feel like they matter. Every group effort of any kind is more productive when the individuals involved feel good about what they're doing.

So let's put things in perspective. Everything that you do matters. Every choice you make has a repercussion. If you make the effort to be the way that you wish everyone else was around you for long enough, you will likely enjoy that group you dreamed of. The waves of intention that you start will inevitably come back to you. When you compliment someone's effort, they work harder. If you can manage to put your dislikes and emotional aches and pains aside, and think positively, your emotional aches and pains will actually subside, and you will in fact enjoy a brighter existence. The fact that our inside thoughts and private ideas about things are actually in some way being received, makes you start policing your own mind and intentions. Being aware of the interconnectivity of things increases your intuitions and successful communication. This increased awareness broadens your consciousness, and enriches your reality.

With all this going on in such a seemingly constant way, it's interesting that we don't find this anywhere in our common curriculum. In the near future, we will see intuition and intention being taught to children as a course in school. This interconnectivity and relationship is the essential missing link to our modern society. We simply can't continue to increase in numbers while having blatant disregard for one another. We have proven ourselves to be quite effective in separating ourselves into a vast array of different groups and teams. But we have yet to prove that we can acknowledge our participation in team human, and find out what real teamwork is. We are technologically and intellectually advanced, yet largely operate in almost medieval social conditions.

Whatever you point your focus and intention toward in your life will manifest in front of you. Whether you think you can or can't, you're correct. Our fear or insecurity can rule and dictate our relationships, and ultimately our lives. Mostly, our fear and insecurities are revolved around our image and pride. When you understand yourself fully you will see that much of that is an illusion. We have slowly and meticulously created the personality that is us. It is always subject to change, every day of your life. We have to assume that is as well for others. We do not have control of circumstances. We do not own rights to anyone's attention or affection. We have no control over other people's actions or reactions. We do, however have complete control over ourselves. In that simple truth anything you can possibly dream can become your destiny. If you can manage to convince yourself that you are capable of achieving that which you desire most, then so you shall. Virtually everything that we do in today's society was at one point considered crazy. Every single idea, tool, material, process, or tradition was the daydream of someone before us. They were convinced that they could create it, and they did.

You can carry a lifetime of hard feelings around with you and they may never be of relevance to anyone else. If your intention is to feel good and enjoy your life to the fullest extent, then certain aspects of the way that you handle yourself in your everyday life start to become clear. Harboring resentment towards anyone for the way things in your life have unfolded is illogical. Repeatedly punishing yourself for mistakes that you made long ago is illogical. Allowing yourself to believe that your choices in the past classify you as a person is illogical. Allowing yourself to be emotionally damaged because things did not transpire around you the way you think they should have is illogical. Allowing yourself to think that while you don't take your own advice, other people should take your advice is illogical. Assuming that the long list of excuses you use for yourself is not applicable to other people's actions around you is illogical. Hating someone for the things that they learned to believe is illogical. Judging yourself by anyone else's standards is illogical. If an individual truly wants peace and joy, then there is no tolerance for resentment, shame, guilt, expectation, offense, contempt, fear, or insecurity. Negative feelings like these simply don't deserve your energy, nor your precious time. We must understand that we cannot actively practice negative intentions and still attain peace. If your mind is occupied with negativity then you are consciously building a perception that will disgust you. If your mind is occupied with positivity you are consciously building a perception that will inspire you. It's that simple.

Sadly, for most people, this whole Constant Telepathic Exchange back and forth is taken as a plague or curse. To be in a public place and be reading and interacting back and forth with other people's opinions and such, without acknowledging it's actual existence, is an unnerving experience. When your intuition is overloaded with a bombardment of people's opinions, it's automatically overwhelming. Both mentally and emotionally. Commonly we would recognize this feeling as anxiety or agoraphobia. If crowds make you nervous, it's likely that you are empathic or hyper aware of your intuitions about people. If you are the kind of person who is processing what someone is thinking about you when they look at you, then being in any setting where more than one person is, will be mentally challenging. Obviously, if you're standing in front of a crowd of people that thinks you are amazing, it is far different then being in front of a crowd full of people that are picking you apart or judging you. However in my experience, once a person who is plagued by this overstimulation becomes aware of why they are unnerved in these situations, and they understand the science of what they're experiencing, it ceases to be scary. It becomes more of an interactive game then a traumatic experience. Of course, it helps that you get to have the confidence of knowing you have insight of a higher perspective of understanding then the crowd around you does. Being aware of this other level of communication gives you a feeling of being gifted in a way. After some practice you will find that this new perspective gives you a sort of intuitive super power.

Another example of how expanding your awareness can abolish or ease fear is being afraid of the dark. Often people are uncomfortable in a completely dark room. Not because there isn't anything to look at, but rather because there seems to be movement and constant excitement in the air around you. As you sit in complete darkness, your eyes adjust to the dark, and you start to see this movement. It could be compared to static on a television or if you have ever tried to take video in the dark. It's unnerving to sit in a room that seems to be packed full of something you have no explanation for... Or a similar affliction that is common in today's society is not being able to sit in a room that is silent. People feel like they need background noise because silence is unnerving to them. Again, it isn't the fact that there's nothing to listen to that bothers us, it's because when there isn't anything to distract your ear you start to notice the deafeningly constant ringing noise that's always there. Similar to darkness, to be seemingly surrounded by something that you have no explanation for is unnerving or scary. In both situations, what makes us uncomfortable is the unidentified ambient energy that surrounds us. Or rather, not having an understanding of what it is. Every object operates on a harmonic frequency. A sound is actually emitted off of a stone or a book. While the frequency coming off of any particular object may not be audible to you, once it resonates with the multitude of other frequencies that are around us, it becomes part of a symphony of vibrating energy and matter. There is swirling movement of elemental exchange, and a virtual framework of harmonic frequency in the air around us throughout our lives. If you happened to notice this ringing sound and see a doctor, they will explain you have tinnitus. They call it a malfunction of the processing of vibrations in the eardrum... Despite there being scientific evidence of an actual constant harmonic vibration around us. Ironically, tinnitus is most common in musicians, people with perfect pitch, or in countries where their language is tone-specific. When information is sent back and forth from satellites to cell phones, or television or radio towers to devices, it is sent in the form of a harmonic frequency with specific tonal and coding variables. All of these signals are "broadcast" in a general direction, they are not aimed in a beam directly to your device. What this means is that at any moment in your day there can be hundreds of different harmonic frequencies crossing paths and inevitably reaching your ear. In some places people are being diagnosed with something they are calling "frequency sensitivity". These people are bothered by the framework of data and frequency in the air around us, and have even resigned to living in caves high in the mountains to find a reprieve from the constant noise. Much like any other extrasensory perception, we all experience these things to one extent or another, usually unknowingly.

Now that we have broadened our perception of what is going on when discussing our well-being, the importance of that perception and the intention we project become more evident. If you can manage to maneuver through your life in a relatively fearless and inspired way, you will find yourself to be a far more effective individual. Making it a practice to have your mind and thoughts supporting your intention in the world is what is known as alignment. Being that all of your energy in the day is focused towards a certain goal or outcome. Usually, our energy is divided amongst any one of what seem to be a thousand different directives or directions in our day. This makes it unlikely for us to achieve any particular goal, as it only receives a portion of our effort. If all you wanted was food, you would find it. If all you wanted was shelter, you would find it. Similarly, if all you want is peace, you will find it. If you daydream about having a peaceful life, but spend your time complaining about everything that's wrong with your surroundings, peace will likely continue to elude you. When you have received some form of good news, and you wake up excited to have a great day, regardless of what circumstances fall before you, you will have a great day. You take it in stride and continue to focus your attention on the goal ahead. Having a focus of something inspiring on the horizon makes obstacles seem trivial. Whoever you are, wherever you find yourself, you have the ability to program your perception of things to support a feeling of contentment or satisfaction. You also have the ability to be completely disgusted with the way things are.

How you narrate the circumstances that fall before you in your inner dialogue determines the effect your circumstances have on you. The intentions that you project determine your character, and help to build the experience that you subconsciously would like to have. Even if you don't explain yourself to anyone, your spiritual and social progression is often quite clear to the aware observer. Those who understand themselves, the interconnectivity that we share, and the power of manifesting your intentions, literally are able to read others like a book. Choose what you would like to portray to the world wisely… like it or not, you are being judged by everyone that encounters you.

Do experiments on your own to verify the validity of this notion. Walk into a grocery store with a general feeling of disgust for mankind. Look at others and judge their actions, presentation, or shortcomings in your head. Take note of how people look at you and interact with you while doing so… Then go back outside, and wait a few minutes. Clear your mind and focus on having faith in mankind. Try to exude positivity and a general sense of care or appreciation. Take note of how differently people look at or interact with you. You will likely notice people stop what they're doing to acknowledge you and greet you. Do this same process in your workplace or home and see what a difference your own outlook makes in the way you are accepted or treated. I have done hundreds of experiments like this and have seen profound validation of the power of intention.

THE SIMPLE UNIVERSE

As I mentioned earlier there are many scientific theories of our existence, but we have yet to find a theory that explains the forces of nature that we experience, the quantum physics that we study, and the reactions we observe in our everyday reality. It can take several years to fully digest all of the leading quantum theories, understand them fully, and understand where they fall short of a full explanation. One day a notion came to me regarding our quantum reality that seamlessly applied to all things, that was so simple it seemed impossible. But after several more years of contemplation and application it became clear that it was not only a plausible, but likely complete explanation to existence in our universe. Historically, the simplest possible solution is correct, and is often found in plain sight. A simple change in perspective can change everything. Allow me to share with you the universe from this perspective…

The universe that we know of is completely full of tiny little bubbles of energy, created by the overabundance of light in the universe. I call these empty containers Anonymous cells. Being a bubble of energy with a void inside makes each Anonymous cell hungry in a sense. Some of them hold matter in the form of protons and neutrons, some of them hold an overabundance of energy, but most remain empty in the endless expanse of space. The purpose of each Anonymous cell is to be occupied. Or simply stated, to have purpose. When it is occupied, the Anonymous cell holds it's cargo tightly, often allowing more protons or neutrons in, but almost never letting them go. When occupied it is automatically attracted to other occupied particles. In this sense, matter is designed to build. When light travels, heat is radiated, or magnetism attracts, it is as well carried by the anonymous cell. This multitude of anonymous cells hold existence in the sense that they make up the canvas that all we observe is painted on. The Anonymous cell is a universal building block that everything that exists is constructed with. This overlooked fundamental building block could potentially be the missing link in our understanding.

It seems that everywhere we look in nature particles are automatically formed in a spherical shape. This is one of the laws that the anonymous cell gives to the construct of nature. Virtually everything we know about our physical world is made up of atoms and photons, and governed by the four forces that are the foundation of our existence. When we look at a picture of an atom we see that the physical portion of the atom is the protons and neutrons that are held within it, but the physical barrier for that atom is the energized Anonymous cell with electrons that encircle that matter. Functionally speaking, when a hammer hits a nail neither the matter of the hammer or the nail actually touch each other. In every form of physical contact the energized cell from one atom to another is the only part that is actually touching. The mind-boggling reality of this is that none of the physical sensations you've experienced in your life had a physical material interaction. It was a relationship of your energy interacting with the energy of everything around you.

Modern physics operates on the notion that there are four main forces that govern the interaction and energy of our universe. **Strong force**, is the force that holds protons and neutrons within an atom. This is hard to imagine when thinking that a few electrons spinning in orbit around the nucleus are holding it all in position, but easily explained when thinking of it as an occupied Anonymous cell. **Weak force**, is the force that slowly deteriorates sound, light, energy, or radio waves in space as it travels. When thinking of space as an empty expanse it is perplexing to try and understand weak Force, but when thinking of space as being full of Anonymous cells that are hungry, it makes perfect sense that waves or beams of energy would deteriorate as they traveled through a sea of hungry containers. **Gravity** is the force that draws physical bodies together. Larger masses draw smaller masses to them. When trying to imagine gravity around you or in space, it's much more logical to understand it as being the cumulative effort of matter and its effort to build. That attraction takes place across a three-dimensional fabric of Anonymous cells. **Electro-magnetism** is a force that occurs usually when constant friction is in place. It creates a secondary field aside from a gravitational pull that draws objects to its source, or holds objects within its field. If we think of electromagnetism as being an invisible flow of charged anonymous cells running through an object like a river, it's easier to envision and understand it's actual process.

Imagining the expanse of the universe as full instead of empty brings several other things to light. First, being the curious fact that most everything travels in waves. Sound travels in space at the same speed and formation as it does under water. Interestingly, it's about three times faster underwater or in space, as it is in our atmosphere. Einstein envisioned the fabric of space as what he called space-time. While this does give a good visual reference of the fabric that holds heavenly bodies in place, it stands to reason that that fabric is a legion of empty cells of energy flowing and moving like an ocean. This perspective as well explains the existence of giant vortices called black holes. This gives solid basis to the notion that they are a drain that flows to an outlet, just as when we see vortices in our physical world. If we imagine that a flame requires empty Anonymous cells to carry the disassembled matter that is it's fuel, (instead of requiring a stream of oxygen as we traditionally have accepted) then suddenly it brings to light the massive burning Suns that are burning throughout the Universe (without an abundance of oxygen.) Each sun acts as a massive 360 degree vacuum. Drawing in from every direction, burning and disassembling matter, and radiating out energy and simple atoms in every direction. This as well gives explanation of why the sun's Corona is hotter than the sun itself, likely being the point where both directions of traffic collide and create enormous friction. Which in turn brings to light why the sun has several magnetic fields. Almost effortlessly you can imagine that the fact that our universe seems to be expanding in every direction is caused by being in an endless sea of hungry Anonymous cells. Like an Alka-Seltzer in a swimming pool we are being slowly drawn out into space. And it's beautiful to know that while doing so, the forces of gravity and electromagnetism will continue to draw things together. If I was to speculate about anything, it would be that the general force of the absorption from the Anonymous collective is slightly less than the force of gravity and electro-magnetism.

Not only does this perspective shed light on our universe on a grand scale, it also sheds light on our observation of quantum physics. Of course, with the makeup and structure of atoms, but as well with our observation of the physical reality in which we live. If you imagine 2 cubic centimeters, one being in front of your face, and the other being out somewhere in the middle of the expanse of space… and picture of that our sun is sending a constant stream of energy through that space. Either in ultraviolet light, or infrared light. The infrared light passes directly through matter, so both the centimeter in front of your face, and the one in the middle of space, receive a similar amount of energy flow for an eternity. This space has energy flowing through it at every moment. Then drawback and imagine that every star in the sky is much like our sun, in the respect that it is sending a constant stream of energy through that same cubic centimeter. You then realize that that single cubic centimeter is receiving a stream of energy from every direction around it, overlapping in multiple layers. You start to understand the magnitude of how jaw-droppingly abundant energy is in the universe. It cannot ever cease, nor any of the matter that is floating and existing within this matrix. Einstein theorized particles of energy he called quanta that would be much like a photon of light, but involved in the flows and waves of energy in every form. This was correct. But it would seem that his theory of the fabric of space time was as well made of what he called quanta.

In each representation of the empty Anonymous cell it is driven to be occupied, have purpose, find balance itself, and attract to each other to sustain as long as possible. It's as though on a particulate level balance is the ultimate directive. Each particle wants to be in a balanced state with positive and negative matter, or (in the case of energy) to be involved in a sustainable flow or current. The constant change of the universe requires that the effort of all of its participants be sustainability. This balance is fundamental. But ironically, change is constant due to the forces of nature.

After you ponder this new perspective for a short time, the actual process of nature in our universe starts to unfold. We reside in a massive ocean of hungry possibility. Everything that is material is drawn together in the effort to build a sustainable existence. Though the universal directive of the forces in control of things seems to be to hold that which is matter together, this attraction creates infinite possibility. Everything that exists used to be something else. It is on its way to becoming something else. The process of change is constant and ubiquitous. Everything is soluble to everything. Energy is in infinite abundance, so wherever action, reaction, life, or existence of any kind should happen, the energy to fuel that endeavor is present. An army of suns and black holes serve as generators and pumps that circulate and recycle all that exists. Every single imaginable possibility for matter will inevitably manifest. We live in a fractal reality. That which is microscopic is similar to that which is vast. Every form of life will inevitably manifest wherever the habitat will allow. Great and small, in every corner of the universe, life will happen. But beautifully, all things will surely cease eventually and become something new. Continuous change and adaptation, eternally. The universe just became an amazingly articulate machine of constant change… that you now can easily understand.

As life-forms struggling for our own survival and well-being in this place, it becomes rather jaw-dropping to imagine that we are a conglomeration of borrowed particles for the purpose of our physical existence. When we cease to live in this body it is relinquished to the collective. A far away sun carries aphoton of energy through billions of miles of space and happens to shine on an apple tree. The leaf of the tree absorbs that energy along with a bit of carbon and sends it to an apple nearby on its branch. You bite into that apple when it falls, and after digesting it, your body sends that carbon molecule to the top of your hand to use as a skin cell. A few days later, you feel a tingle on the top of your hand and brush your other hand across it. Skin cells by the thousands are released from your body. That particular carbon molecule gets caught on a light breeze and carried on the wind 5000 miles to another continent where it lands on a tree. The tree absorbs the carbon along with sunshine to create a cell on the surface of that leaf. That particular carbon cell in the leaf happens to get eaten by a caterpillar that uses it to grow a bit longer. The next afternoon the caterpillar gets eaten by a salamander who digests and uses that particular carbon molecule to rebuild a scrape on its eyeball. The salamander is later eaten by a bird who digests it as it rides air current across the sea before dropping it onto a stone in its feces. The lap of the waves takes it into a water molecule, where it is sucked into the current that carries it to an island in the middle of the sea. It lands finally on the sand, the sun dries out the water, that carbon molecule is released into the air, and the wind currents carry it back to you and you inhale it. Everything is soluble to everything.

A being that is able to understand it's own existence is the most miraculous event that exists in the universe. When intelligent life is able to contemplate and understand it's spiritual existence and the universe around it, the experience of that life is automatically elevated to profound. They become more effective and focused, mindful and patient, acceptant and understanding. We are all made of what was once stardust, and we experience a unique story and circumstances. We have our own struggles and challenges, but to each of us the inevitable goal is to find enlightenment…

ENLIGHTENMENT

As intelligent beings that merely have to participate in the society that we live in, our survival in most parts of the world is relatively a given. We work to provide money for food and shelter primarily. Once that is achieved we work for entertainment, clothes, cars, toys, houses, boats, planes, respect, legacy, and of course satisfaction of every kind. Throughout your day when your mind isn't occupied with work, you have mental free time. For most people this time is largely spent either wrestling with, or trying to distract yourself from the way you "feel" about everything that's going on in your life. Most of us feel absolutely overwhelmed with the barrage of past, present, and future issues, opinions, and obstacles. Most commonly, distraction is the pastime that's preferred. With internet availability, boredom isn't likely. When we're bored all of the things that bother us start to creep into our mind from the corners that we forgot about. We tend to crave anything that can keep our mind off of things. This includes anything from crafts, to drama, to drugs.

The way we "feel" personally subconsciously dictates what kind of experience we are having in our story. Most things that emotionally bother us get played over and over in our minds for a period of time before they're finally put in your bag, still unresolved. As time passes we tend to carry an assortment of different situations and issues that mentally harmed us... and continue to do so. These feelings become part of us. Bearing into consideration that most any of the anger, hatred, violence, or evil that exists in the world is caused by feelings of insecurity, resentment, shame, guilt, and expectation, the bad feelings that we carry are quite literally the enemy. They are a barrier between us and joy, spiritually and emotionally. They are the obstacle that keeps us from enjoying other people's company. They are the poison that ruins our interactions. They cause conflict, alienation, prejudice, anxiety, depression, and war. They are a plague that we share globally that affect our success as an intellectually advanced society. It sounds like the easiest task in the world to go through your day and wear a smile on your face. For most this is difficult, and for some it seems impossible.

Let's use the reference of **ONE SINGLE DAY.** Any random Tuesday that you may or may not recall…

Let's say on this one day you were in a great mood for any reason. You might recall that nothing anyone could do to you that day could've bothered you. You may have felt like you were riding on a cloud, with some kind of emotional armor that made people's reactions or opinions just melt off of you. If you were faced with and angry coworker, you were likely able to diffuse their frustration almost effortlessly. If you found yourself in gridlock traffic, you were patient and it was likely an opportunity to crank up the music and sing at the top of your lungs. If you encountered someone in a snotty mood at the store, you probably we're kind to them anyway. Maybe you talked to your best friend and were able to brighten their day, and made dinner plans. Curiously, you may have as well noticed that people held doors for you, red lights changed for you, and things seemed to just go your way that day…

Now let's say on this day you were instead in a terrible mood for some reason. You might recall that that whole day seemed to tumble on top of you. You may have felt like everything was difficult and irritating. If you were faced with an angry co-worker, you likely gave them a piece of your mind. If you found yourself in gridlock traffic, you were impatient and cut people off, got cussed at a couple times, and it was probably maddening. If you encountered someone in a snotty mood at the store, you may have asked to speak to their manager to report them. You talked to your best friend and they were too preoccupied talking about their life to listen to the bad day you were having, and it irritated you, so you ended the conversation. Of course, people did not hold doors for you, you likely caught every red light, and it probably seemed like nothing could go your way that day....

The overall circumstances of both of those days were likely very similar. Your perspective towards that day was reflective of the mood you were in. So all of your reactions to the circumstances that day were directly affected by that mood. Quite possibly, you either made or lost friends due to that disposition. Your intention and perspective affected everyone around you throughout that day, for the better or worse. Inevitably, the following day you either reaped the benefit or paid the consequence of that days outcome. That one day may have made a long-term affect on your life. You may even rave or lament about that day for years to come. The choices you made in that one day may have set in motion an outcome for your life that you are either dreading or hoping for. To some degree, your choices in that day helped to build how you feel about yourself as a person. You may have said something that day that wounded a long-term relationship with a close friend or family member, and may deal with the repercussions for the rest of your life. Or, you had a meaningful conversation with someone and solidified a friendship that soothes your soul, and lasts the rest of your life.

Using one random day of your life you can see the extent that your mood and disposition towards your experiences can impact your long term well-being. You can either feel like the victim or the recipient of your circumstances, depending on how you feel about yourself. Logically speaking, your emotional well-being and simply feeling good should be your top priority. As it is a multipurpose tool that can manifest the positive outcome of your entire life. This being the case, we must understand that if that is our top priority, then it will naturally be the order of the day. Meaning your primary focus is feeling pleasant as you enter each moment. It makes you patient and tolerant, forgiving and understanding. To carry the priority of feeling good while thinking back on the things in your emotional bag that hurt you, it is simple to apply excuses to people's actions, forgive, and let go. Not to try and free them from guilt, but rather to free yourself from the resentment that you likely carry towards them.

Logic is what allowed me to understand the process of feeling good, and generate a basic outline to deal with emotional baggage. This is done entirely from the perspective that I laid out in the previous chapters. If we are to consider ourselves intelligent beings then that holds us to a certain intellectual standard. Doing things that are emotionally counterproductive or potentially damaging are illogical if you want to feel good...

Shame and guilt- While it is extremely important to learn from our mistakes, being ashamed of ourselves for the mistakes that we've made in the past is not. Being ashamed of yourself is a reaction to the notion that everyone would think less of you if they knew what you had done. This is of course necessary to learn how to behave in the future, but practicing that for a long-term will change the way that you think about you. It can be easy to start to classify yourself as a bad citizen because of the things that you've done in the past. Perpetually justifying you mentally to continue making those choices. Knowing the grand possibility that exists in each day, means that you can always change your destiny. But you have to be able to let go of the shame in order to take on a new perspective about yourself. You literally cannot feel good if you feel bad about yourself. Guilt is similar, but guilt is usually the prequel to shame. You feel guilty when you are worried someone will find out what you have done, and you feel ashamed once they have. Wearing guilt for any length of time starts to make an individual keep their true self hidden, and operate on a superficial personality when they are around people. Often spending most of their time in solitude. Shame and guilt lead directly to not caring.

I recall having a conversation with some friends when I was about 10 years old, where we were talking about God and the naughty things we had done. A friend who went to bible school told me that I was probably going to go to hell when I die. This kid was more educated on the subject that I was, so I took what he said as fact. The shame and guilt that I carried from that conversation affected a lot of my choices in the following decade. I assumed that since I was already damned, that whatever else I did from this point didn't much matter. So for a while I did whatever I felt like, regardless of the repercussions. I was mean to people for fun, and enjoyed manipulating others to get my way. Naturally, I lied, cheated, and even stole whenever I saw fit. My world revolved around looking cool and getting my way. As you might guess, I found myself at a certain point with no close friends, and fate put me in a situation where I lost everything that meant something to me. At that time I felt worthless. I didn't have anything positive to look back on to find worth or take pride in. There was no one to turn to for help, and I found myself alone. As I sat and contemplated suicide, it occurred to me that none of the situation that existed in my life **had** to be that way. I could have made different choices throughout, and be sitting in an entirely different situation. In that moment, the possibility of a different kind of life and feeling talked me out of giving up. I went to sleep that night sobbing, and woke up the next morning, started letting go of the shame and guilt that I carried, and decided that my path to enlightenment had begun long before. I saw that whole duration of time where I lived life in a wounded state as insight to what I see in other people. I started to understand why people make the choices they do and harmed each other.

Expectation- Intellectually, it's hard to hold people to any particular standard. The nature of being intelligent means that you have the ability to decide how people "should" react to situations. When you find that they don't react the way you were hoping, it can bother you to your core. When you have expectations for the outcome of situations, people's reactions can drive you insane, if you let them. But holding people to an expectation is assuming that they are going to be in a similar mindset to you, and see your logic. In this convoluted society, that's not likely. If you are smart enough to see how people "should" act and react to things, then you are also smart enough to know how "likely" you think those things are. You may find yourself expecting a person to react a certain way, despite the fact that you already know they most likely won't.

There are millions of people that are so bothered by the way things "should be" that they do not enjoy the good fortune they have. We all have a history, and are all at a point in our escalation of understanding that is specific to us. Whatever mood we are in effects our decisions, as we know. Trying to have a particular expectation for a person is like gambling. You are putting your hopes on a particular outcome that may or may not transpire. Logically, the level of loss you can experience from any bet is relative to the size of your wager. Emotionally speaking, if you find yourself angry or frustrated with someone's choices, you were gambling too much on something that wasn't a sure thing. If your hope was the currency that you as well used to feed your family, would you have bet as highly on that outcome? Most likely the answer is no. You should know however, that in terms of energy and attention, it is an equal value. If you allow an outcome of a situation to put you in a terrible mood, everyone that depends on you is going to pay the price while that mood continues. Your energy and patience will be less for everything else that happens while you wear that mood. Just as we saw in the example of that "one day," why you got put into a certain mood may be irrelevant once the dust has cleared from your reactions because of it. While you have successfully managed to afford your house and bills that month, it may have cost a truckload of joy and quality time.

To truly protect your well-being you must make it your prime directive. When you set off into your day it should be as though you are in the best of moods. If you can manage to not need to be satisfied by your day, rather you are satisfied already and the outcome of the day is your entertainment. Keeping the right perspective on things changes the entire dynamic of a conversation, a day, a friendship. Being understanding enough to not have expectations of the people you share company with, will ensure longstanding relationships and cultivate a feeling of contentment throughout your days.

Resentment- We live together in a crowded and busy society where we are raised to judge ourselves by comparison. We live by opinion. Our own opinion of ourselves is based on everyone else's opinion of us. We didn't have any idea whether or not we were pretty or ugly until someone told us. It is truly difficult to try and find yourself, along with the respect and satisfaction that you desire in this judgmental place. Most people want to be noticed really bad. Everybody wants to be noteworthy in one way or another. Either for beauty, athletic ability, strength, speed, intelligence, artistic ability, music talent, work ethic, juggling, etc. And if you don't happen to be the best at one of those sought-after positions, then you can always try your hand at sarcasm, toughness, coolness, humor, or sympathy as a last resort. In one way or another everybody wants to be noticed and recognized a certain way. We protect our image with our lives. People do crazy things to protect their name or legacy. It's easy to resent people who are gifted, talented, popular, or even famous. We assume these people have an easier time and are enjoying life more than us. We tend to resent in a certain way those who have been given an opportunity that we haven't.

Resentment is like inflicting a constant reoccurring ailment on yourself, with the intent of having it harm someone else. It is like blaming someone else for the circumstance of your life. Often when you carry resentment for someone they are either oblivious to it, or don't care. Even if they are aware of it intimately, there's nothing they can say to soothe that feeling. Ultimately, it resides in your mind only. It is a constant emotional ache that your perspective causes you. The simple truth of resentment is that a person's ability to have joy and shine within their own means surpasses how fortunate they are. Most likely, those who you resent for having opportunities that you don't are no closer to contentment or satisfaction then you are. Historically speaking, fame, fortune, and control tend to come with pressure, responsibility, and stress, and have a troubling and negative effect on a person's well-being. Ironically, someone out there has resentment toward you for the gifts you likely take for granted..

Whoever and wherever you are, you have the ability to arrange your affairs in a way that suits you, and find a perspective that elates you. One where you are thankful and appreciative of the gifts you have in your life, and are satisfied completely with your current path. Count your blessings. I watched a story about a boy who was born with a disease that covered his entire body in scabs. They would crack open and bleed anywhere his body moved. He lived in constant pain. There was no cure for the condition, and the boy was growing up at home. He wanted to go to public school like the rest of the kids, but his parents advised against it. When he was finally able to go to school, of course the reaction of exasperation was unanimous. But the boys positive and helpful attitude quickly won over the school. He was known to always put others first and help people with their struggles, because he understood how tough life could be. People are born with or endure insurmountable odds, and still manage to persevere and be an example to others. People without homes, people without legs, people without sight, people who don't have a friend, people who have never been in love, people who don't know where their next meal will come from, people who are afraid for their lives every day, people who manage to rise above their situation and be an example to others. Amazingly, these people take a story of their life that could have been tragic and sad, and turn it into something that is inspiring and uplifting. Bearing into consideration that of all of the places you could have been born into, do you still feel like a victim of your circumstances? Is there a justified reason why you would want to inflict yourself with the burden of resentment? For me, the answer was no.

Self-doubt- Fear will keep you from doing anything amazing in your life. Doubting your capabilities in the face of future obstacles is illogical. Thus far, you have somewhat successfully navigated through (how ever many years old you are) of life's obstacles. There is no reason to assume the worst possible scenario will occur and you'll fail in the face of it. However, through the power of intention you will manifest that situation and fail as you predicted, if you envision it enough. The power of intention is quite possibly limitless. We surprise ourselves over and over in life, doing things we previously would've bet we could never do. I've pushed myself far past what I thought my limit was. Each time it was because I was determined to reach a goal or fulfill a responsibility. As far as I've pushed myself I still felt like I had more to give. Always. I would guess the same for you.

When a person is put into a dire situation that is perhaps life threatening to them or others, It Is frequent for those people to display superhuman strength or capability. In these situations it is the determination that a person has for that outcome that makes it possible for them to achieve what they would have thought impossible. No was not an option. If you see your child getting crushed by a car, even though logic says you shouldn't be able to, you find yourself able to lift the vehicle and are able to save your child. When a person has complete faith they are protected by god amidst danger, they see impossible good luck or resilience.

When a holy man meditates for two weeks without water or sleep. When a church full of people are convinced their prayers will heal someone that's ill, and they are suddenly better. Clearly, there are some incredible capabilities that remain unused in each and every one of us. The prerequisite for being able to use them is that you must have conviction. If you need to cross a log over a river and are sure you're going to fall, guess what... if you think you're going to freeze when the girl you like talks to you, guess what.. if you think you aren't a good enough person to find happiness... guess what?

You are a walking miracle of limitless possibility. Most anything that you can put your mind to, and have conviction for, you can achieve. People just like you climb to mountain peaks that are above the clouds, because they are convinced that they can. People just like you single-handedly start businesses, foundations, charitable organizations, etc, because they're convinced they can or have to. People with no motivation to speak of get inspired by something, and wake up one day with Ironclad motivation to get things done. The determining factor with any of these people is that they have convinced themselves that there's a need or desire that they must fill. The prospect of your life having a grand purpose of any sort is motivational enough to carry you across deserts, through battle, and up from rock bottom.

Hate- There are many forms of hatred practiced around our globe. Most of which are not directed at a single person, because we have the automatic tendency of trying to make general judgments across a whole group once we're offended by one. Usually hate derives from great Injustice, resentment, expectation, fear, or disgust. But hate can as well be extended for many reasons like race, religion, belief system, political views, geographic location, sports teams, people with red cars, people who sag their pants, people who use the word "like" too often, or literally any other difference you can think of. People practice hate like a hobby. People deliberately surf the Internet to step on ideas, disrupt conversations, and irritate or anger anyone that catches their attention. There are as well people who do this in their everyday life. Peeking out their window and talking under their breath about every single person that passes them, for some reason or another. Individuals who look for any reason they can find to make fun of or hate others for. Obviously, these type of people have been wounded by life in such a way that they have lost their own desire for well-being. They have given up on trying to feel good, and they have succumb to the second-rate form of satisfaction you get for being able to ruin someone's day. Most of the hate we carry was taught to us by someone else. Much of the hatred that exists today is derived from a time before now. It's passed down like a tradition, and people take it as a personality trait. I've heard people say "my family hates Irish people." Or "my whole family hates black people." Both statements are absurd. If you're trying to support an argument in order to fit into a family or group you're plenty smart enough to find reasons to feel justified. So here you have the family of people that are creating an assumed adaptation that will inevitably keep them from feeling complete. Does the 3rd or 4th generation child that's born into this family actually choose that disposition, or are they justifying it in order to follow suit?

Logically, we all understand that hatred is unhealthy baggage to carry. We know it's often childish and ignorant to generalize a race or style of people from the experience of a few. If your effort is to feel good about yourself and the world around you, there is no room for hatred in your mind. You relent to assume that each of those people who have done you wrong were doing so to protect their image, or because of resentment, or because they were afraid, or because they were just having the negative version of "that one day." Having hatred and ugly feelings on your mind while you live your life causes you to make poor decisions. Most of the time we regret these poor decisions we make, but we often justify them as soon as they happen. When dealing with all situations, the enlightened individual will automatically forgive people's ugly actions. You mentally offer them an excuse or justification for why they acted the way they did, so you don't have to carry the burden of hatred. Enlightenment is entirely about self-care and preservation.

Change- We are meant to change over time. Our abilities change, our outlooks change, our directives and goals change. What's important to us changes. I often see people who avoid change to uphold an image that they have built for themselves. Like they picked a certain part of their story and declared this is "who I am." For these people trying to upgrade or adapt as time goes on becomes an intellectual struggle, because they feel they are not being true to themselves if they seek change. Of course, logically this doesn't stand to reason. Most likely, you are the 5.0 version of who you were long ago. There were ideals, personality traits, and directives that became outdated and no longer served your purposes. So you ran a new program that was more streamline to your ambitions. In a sense, changing your attitude or personality can be like standing on your rooftop and shouting out to your neighbors that you were wrong before. Of course, you don't ever have to do that. But intellectually that's what it feels like when you're about to make a substantial change. Nevertheless, it is necessary in order to advance.

As we've learned, change is the order of existence. Everything that exists is on its way to becoming something else. Similarly, you are on your way to becoming someone else. Change will be necessary. Admitting you were wrong is necessary. Escaping from others opinions of you and what you do is necessary, if you intend to evolve over time. Really, evolution is the effort of all life. We are born with a specific coding of characteristics, dispositions, and personality traits. This is a somewhat random collage of both our parents, programmed on our DNA. (This would be the portion of our DNA coding that biologists would call "junk DNA", as they do not see that it relates to our physical characteristics and have yet to embrace it having to do with our social characteristics.)

Throughout our lives, as we face our struggles in trying to adapt to this changing world, we make upgrades. Sometimes these upgrades are physical talents, but in our quickly changing society as humans, most of our upgrades are social changes. If you had a child at a young age, and a child later in life. Likely these two children differed in certain ways. The child you had at a young age is likely very similar to the kind of person that you were at that time. The child that was born later in your life most likely was born with the social adaptations that you have made since having the first one. Traditionally speaking, the youngest child is usually the most innovative, unique, and emotionally or intellectually stable.

Change is the nature of life. Things are not created in order to remain the same. When you make change for yourself people will understand. If they don't, then they themselves are afraid of growth. If the changes that you make for yourself are logical and sound enough, others will follow suit. The people that you may have been concerned with judging your choices, see the merit in the upgrades you have made, and make those changes for themselves. It's frequent that you see someone make a positive change for themselves and within a short time they have influenced those around them to make the same changes. It's quite clear to see that this is the construct of evolution. Life-forms are constantly changing to adapt to a constantly changing world, in a constantly changing universe. Threats change, responsibilities change, and as we are seeing in recent times the nature of engagement as well changes. The changes we make as individuals sometimes influence the entire group, and become a permanent alteration in the DNA of our species. The crowd wisdom that we share decides the applicability and outcome of any of our individual adaptations. Beautifully, no single opinion can determine which traits become species-wide, and which die off with their creators.

You see, enlightenment is a matter of designing a perspective that allows you to be free of weight. It's about not needing to carry baggage of any kind. You will never be able to change the world to your liking. You may not even be able to change your corner of the world in that respect. You can however, change your perception of the world to your liking. If you are convinced that things are exactly the way they should be at this time, then you are not harmed by the condition of things. You don't have a preference of how the day unfolds. When people act out and say rude or hateful things to you, you respond with something productive. You are thankful and appreciative of the experience of your life, and you carry a satisfaction for how you are living it. Enlightenment is about making your primary focus your own well-being. Once a person reaches a point in their conception of themselves where they feel that they understand and embrace the individual that they are, then they are able to understand others in a profound and similar way. While we may not have insight as to where someone is from, nor their direction, we can clearly see that they are on a path similar to ours. They are likely wrestling with the same feelings that we either have had, currently have, or will have. The enlightened mind is able to choose wisely in our own affairs, and influence others to do the same.

Peace and enlightenment are much like a martial art. They must be learned first, then practiced for long enough that it becomes second nature. Before long you do not have to try to be peaceful, you just are. You have at that point successfully manifested your intentions for yourself. The confidence and conviction that that feeling awards you is invaluable. When you are on this path you are a more effective version of what you used to be. In every possible situation of your life you are able to connect fully, express yourself productively, and physically achieve things that were previously out of your reach. You'll find your focus and attention are crisp and precise. Your thoughts and intentions will be amplified to those you know. Your intuition and insight to things will as well be amplified. Your perception supports the way you want to think, your thoughts support the way you want to feel, your feelings support the way you want to act, the way you act supports the direction that you want to go, and the destination you are going is enlightenment. Full circle deliberate and positive living. If you reach this feeling of enlightenment you will likely have a hard time explaining it to others, but the saving grace of such a thing is that you don't need to explain it to anyone. They can see in your example the way that they want to feel. To be spiritually aware and engaged in this way, you are evolving to a higher adaptation. And again, logically speaking, this higher perception and state of being is the next evolutionary step for mankind. Just imagine how productive and efficient humanity's efforts will be when enlightenment is the new fad.

Meditation- your brain is like the playground that your mind plays on. Most of the time, your mind runs on impulse or autopilot. For most people, your mind kind of bounces around from one topic to the next. It can even be difficult to choose just one of those thoughts to focus on without being distracted by the meandering of your autopilot mind. You may even feel like there's something wrong with your mind, because of its constant inability to focus. This inability to focus causes stress and anxiety, and can be maddening to a person. In moments of clarity it's as though you take the wheel of the ship that is your mind, and are able to steer or focus your energy towards a single thought. In these moments you may find that you are surprised or impressed with how effective your mind can be.

Meditation is the practice of focus. There are many different forms of meditation practiced around the world. All of them are a matter of pinpointing your focus to a particular sensation or thought. What this practice does is exercising your consciousness to have control over yourself. As with all exercise, the more you do it the stronger and more skilled you become. The main objective of meditation is peace and a sense of mindfulness. Being able to have a vivid awareness of a singular moment and the sensations involved is mindfulness. Scientific studies have shown that through meditation and mindfulness a person can actually change the function of their brain. Regular practice can increase your focus and effectiveness towards virtually everything in your life. Being aware of the sensation of your existence in any situation grants you the ability to either be vividly present, or safely withdrawn, depending on your intention. A mind that practices meditation regularly will be more peaceful, confident, decided, aware, patient, thoughtful, and likely more satisfied with the experience of their life.

It has been shown that through focus and meditation a person can overcome physical distractions or discomforts. One can maintain a feeling of calmness in stressed situations. There have even been cases where people are able to remedy physical and intellectual ailments simply by directing their focus to do so. The autopilot orchestration of your mind and body is amazing by itself, but when your conscious mind is able to focus and direct that activity, the result is incredible and satisfying. Ironically, through the practice of mindful existence within yourself you can in fact transcend the limits of your conscious mind. Often times, a person who is skilled at meditation can find a perception where they are vividly aware of the orchestration of life on a grand scale, and their own ego or identity becomes irrelevant. Being able to step outside of your own objectives, even for a moment, can be a life-changing experience.

Meditation as an individual is a valuable tool to your life and well-being. Group meditation amplifies the intention of each individual participating. Many schools around the world now have begun to have the students practice meditation as a group. There are even mindfulness classes that some of the students participate in. The effect that this has on the students as individuals is profound. Not only are they better and more effective at their own studies, but the children tend to have more patience and confidence in other areas of their lives. The students as a group tend to get along better as well. Sharing a sense of camaraderie for having experienced something both within themselves, and outside of themselves. Meditation relieves stress and anxiety, and cultivates a sense of well-being. As far as your emotional and intellectual well-being is concerned, meditation and mindfulness is the most important art to practice, or even master.

HIGHER POWER

Trying to speak of a higher power is difficult because most of what we can possibly say about it can be argued from a different perspective. Many religions believe there is only one God. Some of them believe there are many gods. Some believe that nature itself is the higher power. Many believe that if you worship the wrong God you will be punished. Some of them believe that we, the beings of this planet, are gods ourselves. Some religions believe that a higher power decides our fate when we die. Some believe that a higher power is merely the overseer and orchestrator of our lives. Most religions agree that there is a force in all things that governs our lives to one extent or another. That we are able to develop a relationship and understanding with that force. Once we do, we are granted insight and conviction. It's generally thought that if you have faith in the power of that force, it will somehow protect you throughout your life. It will help you make tough choices, give you strength in the face adversity, and if you are true and devout enough, it will fill your being and lift you to a higher awareness.

Throughout all of these religions it as well seems to be generally accepted that the more time you spend in praise or recognition of that force, the more closely you understand your own life and the others around you. Prayer and meditation seem to be the main pathways to building that relationship. However, in some beliefs song, enduring pain, repetitious chanting, drug-induced states, great sacrifice, and certain tests of will can as well bring you closer to that higher power. In each instance, it is clear that the method of getting closer to the higher power is disassociating yourself with your human desires or comforts. Usually, if a person has developed a relationship with a higher power, they are not likely concerned with their image. Nor are they concerned with money, power, status, sex, or any of the physical pleasures of man. In order to put ourselves aside, we need to feel a certain satisfaction. As humans our wants and desires are many. An individual must have already attained a satisfaction or contentment within themselves, before they can simply let go of their ego. To a large degree, all that we desire outside ourselves is in effort to fill the void of satisfaction we have within ourselves.

In a sense, satisfaction is the goal in this life. If you are lucky enough to find satisfaction and contentment before you pass, you have won the lottery of fate. As you will inevitably pass in peace. What happens to us when we die is certainly up for debate as well, but its universally believed that having peace before you do is the goal. Many of the religions depict the afterlife as a period of reconciliation for the life we just finished living. Either on your own accord or administered by a judge of some form or another. Whether it is the case that we either go to heaven or hell, the seven layers of Heaven, if we reincarnate, or even if our body merely goes into the Earth and is decomposed, the effort to find peace and enlightenment has definite merit. All things considered, whatever our fate is, it stands to reason that being on your best behavior during this life enhances your experience, leaves the best legacy and example possible for those who you love, and ensures your individual fate in the afterlife.

We may never actually know whether or not we have a creator to thank for these lives that we enjoy on this beautiful planet, but it seems to be the case that mankind has received instruction or Insight from beings that are more advanced than ourselves at certain times in history. Virtually every ancient culture on the planet tells of a history of interaction or education that we as humans have received from visitors from somewhere else. Until such time as they stop back by to settle the dispute, the order of deciding who it was is irrelevant. It is an intellectual gamble to choose one of the particular gods described by one of the religions. It is a leap of faith, if you will. Nevertheless, believing that there is at least someone that is more advanced and wiser than ourselves in control over things can be comforting. Would it matter much to you if it was found that God was an old bearded man, or a little grey alien? Once we pass we will all know for sure. But there may never be a way for us to put a face to the name or notion of God.

In my perspective, all of our thoughts and intentions are delivered back and forth to one another in the form of energy across the fabric of the universe. It seems that all of these individual thoughts and intentions combine to form a collective wisdom that surrounds us. It seems that whatever information you may be looking for spiritually, it is available to you at any time, any place around the world. Information and feeling seem to be readily available to whoever seeks it with conviction. If you want insight on what choice to make for a situation in your life, it seems that you merely need to ask. If you are looking for direction on where to go, you merely ask. If you want more strength, patience, forgiveness, compassion, you merely need to ask for it. Government agencies have been able to do tests with individuals that do remote viewing. They were taken to a remote or enclosed space and asked about a particular place in a far-off country that they've never been. These remote viewers are able to draw a picture of how buildings are arranged in this place, where roads lead, how many people are there, and explain what the activity is that's going on in that place. A spiritual medium can hold an object that belonged to someone that is missing, and have a clear vision where on the planet is that person is, whether or not they're still alive, what happened to them, and in some cases exactly where their body was buried after they passed. Recently, a medium was able to see where a missing boy was, who he was with, and even have insight to what day they would be arriving at a particular grocery store in a another state, even the clothes they would be wearing… They sent authorities to that grocery store in plain clothes to wait and see if they showed up when the medium predicted. In walks the exact woman that the medium described, and the boy that had been missing, wearing the clothes that were predicted. It seems that there is no limit to how far our intuition and insight can reach.

People all over the world seem to sense things that are outside of their applicable knowledge. When they asked for it, they are able to have insight or information that they "shouldn't" be able to know. Past, present, or future. I cannot say for sure whether or not the information that a person seeks is merely picked up by their mind like a signal, if the information is hand-delivered by angels, or if God is granting you that info. But it is quite clear that it is available to you. A collective consciousness that surrounds us. Furthermore, it seems that your thoughts and activities are recorded on the items that you touch and come in contact with throughout your day. It has been shown many times by mediums that hold an object that is hundreds of years old, that they can have insight as to how that object was used, and by who. Hundreds of years after person has passed someone is able to catch glimpses of what they did in their life by holding an object that that person once held. It can be either eerie or inspiring to know that if a person is in-tune with you somehow, they may be able to see what and how you are currently doing, and your actions in this life will echo throughout history.

In my best description, the higher power that we all speak of is the conglomerative network of energy that we all share. It is very much responsible for the lives that we are given. If you believe in it wholeheartedly, the experience of your life will be enhanced. When you need help or insight, you merely need to ask and it will be provided. It delivers your intentions wherever you would like them to go. The more you understand its magnificent power and expanse, the more trivial the tribulations of your life become. It can guide and protect you, if you are connected to it consciously. When you pass, you become a small piece of this grand design, and the pure truth the life you just finished becomes clear. You have an elevated insight from which to understand and make peace with your choices throughout. After you have found peace with your life, it seems that some may go on to heaven, some linger in the effort to help loved ones, and some seem to be reborn seeking another chance. Your soul seems to be a mass of energy that vibrates on a harmonic frequency that is specific to you. That harmonic frequency is what binds your souls energy together, differentiates your intentions from everyone else's, and even makes you recognizable to familiar souls in the afterlife or if you reincarnate.

Reincarnation is still a topic for debate. However there have been thousands of confirmed cases where children tell of who they were in a previous life, how they died, who their family members were, what they did for a living, and specific details of their lives and families. In many cases these children even know what their names where, where they lived, and their stories are confirmed to be verified with news stories or the actual families that lost that person. In many cases, children will instantly pick up an instrument or tool and know how to use or play specific songs with no instruction. Many medical professionals have diverted from their mainstream field of study to specializing in the study of afterlife or reincarnation. There are cases in every corner of the world that have validated the belief in reincarnation for people that were skeptics otherwise. Even for those that were raised in a religion that was against the idea. In many studies individuals had verifiable stories of as many as 15 previous lives before their current one. Whether you believe or not, there is convincing evidence to suggest that our souls may revisit this world at different times, as different people. Inevitably with different lessons to learn in those lives. This notion validates the feeling that some people seem familiar to you when you first meet them. Our lives seem to be more of ongoing story that spans across time, rather than a brief chapter in the story of mankind.

If there is a being or beings that are in control or orchestration of life on this planet, they inevitably operate on this network of energy and intention. Our own intuition operates on this scale as well. Both past and future possible outcomes seem to be available to those who are looking. We see glimpses of possibility and make choices in favor of the outcomes we desire. Often we exactly predict people's actions or words long before the event transpires. We forecast these conversations or events and decide whether or not to follow through with certain choices as though time itself is an overlapping circular format, instead of a linear format. We seem to be directed to certain people or experiences, and even guided away from some of them. It's possible this is merely done by our intuition, or perhaps by an entity outside ourselves. Uncanny coincidences happen all over the planet in every moment. If there is a singular being that orchestrates these trillions of different possibilities, and guides each of us here on earth to our destiny, the task and upkeep would be virtually unfathomable. But there definitely seems to be an orchestration to each of our lives that exceeds our individual perception of our own fate.

From a religious standpoint, this may or may not validate your faith. From a scientific standpoint, this may offer you an applicable construct to existence, despite mainstream science being guarded against anything that isn't physically observable. If you previously had no faith in anything, perhaps this perspective has given you something plausible to have faith in. Whatever your belief, background, or spiritual path, (if any), there is a very real existence to our interconnected relationship with each other. This being the case, there is a definite cause to try and be a decent person, seek peace in your life, and spread joy the best you can. If for no other reason than your own satisfaction or destiny. We make the bed we lie in, so if we're uncomfortable in that bed and we aren't trying to make it better, then we are openly accepting discomfort for our lives, and inevitably our destiny or karma .

COMMON THREADZ

Somewhere out there in our society, there is a group or organization in place to support any particular idea, belief, or affliction that you can possibly imagine. We have become intelligent enough to provide a convincing supporting argument to virtually anything that can be dreamt up. We have drawn lines of separation on the earth and between each other that continue to hinder our advancement as a civilization. There is an endless number of things that we can all disagree on, and fight to the death over. But virtually none of it is productive to us as individuals, nor as a civilization. Despite being in an intellectually and technologically-advanced society, we hold dearly to ancient arguments and differences. The reality that we share is that we are all strikingly similar to each other, and are struggling in the same situation as each other. Most of us feel alone in our perception of reality, and most of us long for a sense of community… together.

Whether we choose to acknowledge it or not, we are all part of a team working towards a common goal. We are trying to orchestrate and manage our civilization in such a way that it creates a better life for ourselves and future generations. One that supports the advancement of our species. The eventual goal that we seem to be dragging our feet toward is unity. In all of our recorded history, there has never been a time where mankind operated as a unified force. Our entire history is riddled with discord. It has become obvious that in all of our separation we have created a society where there is no standard of interaction. People do terrible things to one another, because of their differences, with the support of the masses. We are perpetually justified by our acts of segregation as being "normal." The redundant exchange of all of this fighting and argument happens **while** we are mis-managing our resources, and leaving and messy and damaged Earth for the next generations to clean up. There are current and urgent matters that need our cumulative attention that are left on the back burner, because we are preoccupied bickering about our differences.

The following list is an effort to find a social basis of some sort. An intellectual and spiritual common ground that can be shared by everyone, regardless of their beliefs. It is a list of 50 common threadz that are subtly shared throughout humanity. Some have to do with the intellectual or spiritual well-being of mankind, and some have to do with the governing of mankind. This list is meant to be a poll that is to be publicly taken by the influential people in our world. This includes heads of the scientific community, as well as the religious community. It will as well be open to the public through a website where people will sign in with their first name, hometown, and religious belief, if any. They will get a statistic result once they've completed the poll. One that shows them how many people in their area or globally share their same opinions, and from what different faiths'. The end result will be that after a few million people have participated, there will be hopefully at least a small few of these common threadz that were unanimously agreed upon. Once we have reached that list, it will be broadcast as a common ground for Humanity. This list can achieve what would be impossible around a conference table. It has the potential to bridge gaps between all of the belief systems that we have divided ourselves into.

Great contemplation and care has been put into the compilation of this list. It is a delicate process to create statements that hold us all to an intellectual or spiritual standard, without offending anyone's belief system. The effort is to have as many of these common threadz stand the test of time. In that respect, I have made no mention of things that I know cannot be agreed upon at this time. These simple common threadz are not openly discussed, and need to be. In order for this movement to succeed, the people that participate will need to want unity of some kind. They will have to be genuinely tired of the fear, hate, and insecurities we all share. Inevitably, throughout this process we will find out if mankind is truly ready to move forward as a team.

1. The ability to change our environment in any way gives us the responsibility to cultivate it thoughtfully.
2. The point of procreation is to create offspring that are better than we are.
3. We have an intellectual responsibility to enhance our quality of life, and broaden public awareness with the knowledge we gain.
4. There is a certain existence to each human spirit before and after this life.
5. Whether you think you can or can't, you're right. Your beliefs and intentions govern your abilities.
6. There have been influences through our history that exceed our human ability or knowledge.
7. Industry should be thoughtfully and sustainably carried out. Disregard for the environment in industrial or agricultural practice is a crime against nature, as the potential impact can't be predicted.
8. Treat others with the same respect and kindness that you wish to receive. By doing so, you enhance the quality of your own life.
9. Well-being can be affected by prayer or intention.

10. The object of life is to find understanding and contentment, and share it with those who still struggle.

11. Peace, contentment, or Enlightenment is the goal of leading a good life.

12. Divine power can be observed as the wellspring of energy that fuels existence.

13. Your thoughts and intentions are the foundation of your character, your choices and actions are manifested intentions.

14. All conflict should be able to be resolved without violence. Violence of any kind is the tool of intellectual or social failure.

15. Fear is caused by a lack of confidence and can be absolved through understanding, empowerment, or faith.

16. The primary goal of any governing institution should be the health, safety, and well-being of its citizens.

17. Satisfaction or contentment cannot be measured through wealth or possessions. Greed is admitting your insecurity is a priority over others.

18. It's never too late for change. Your condition is not your conclusion.

19. Public leaders should be wise, patient, and thoughtful in dealing with matters that affect their citizens.

20. Peace, patience, forgiveness, humility, generosity, and appreciation are productive practices.

21. We are still learning the universe around us. We in fact, don't know everything.

22. Correcting mistakes, paying due penalty, or apologizing ensures the positive impact and growth for you and the affected person(s).

23. All life-forms great and small seem to possess a conscious awareness and state of well-being. Peace helps all life flourish, turmoil hinders it.

24. Although we as individuals are noticeably different from one another, we are strikingly similar in many ways.

25. Some are gifted, some are hindered, but the ability to shine within your own means surpasses how fortunate you are.

26. Life is simple in its essence. Distractions and attachments make seeing the simplicity of life difficult.

27. The best food for the human body is naturally found or produced. Quality of food should never be sacrificed for shelf life or profitability.

28. Society is a team effort, in that respect the success of any country can be seen in its poorest citizens.

29. Crime is reflective of the general desperation of a community. Enhance the quality of life and people react accordingly.

30. Conflict is often caused by fear, greed, or insecurity. One who is confident and content is rarely in conflict.

31. Telepathy, telekinesis, remote viewing, the power of prayer, intuition, and cumulative consciousness are scientifically documented human abilities or that are practiced and utilized around the world. Intuition and intention should be part of our curriculum.

32. Deliberately mis-educating citizens to serve your own agenda shows you are not serving your community.

33. The general public needs to be kept better informed of the matters of their community, environment, and government. Advancement flourishes when everyone is informed.

34. Unity is an unsurpassable step in the evolution of mankind. Division and discord harms the success of any team effort.

35. People are most efficient and productive when they feel like they are part of a team effort.

36. Every being is a community of living cells within a confined space, working together for the purpose of that beings health. This should be the model for our society.

37. The only constant in the universe is change. Our ability to adapt to change determines our success in this world.

38. Following trends is your pre-programmed instinct. To enhance or start new trends shows your evolution and conscious involvement.

39. If your mind is filled with hate and anger you are consciously building a perception that will disgust you.

40. The most productive debates are handled calmly. Thoughtful words are far more impactful than loud ones.

41. History should always be protected in its actual story. Covering parts of history ensures those mistakes will be repeated.

42. Native cultures should be protected from expansion or social dilution. Indigenous cultures and languages must be preserved.

43. Resentment is like blaming someone else for your condition or situation. It is of no benefit to you.

44. One of the greatest achievements you can find in this life is to inspire others to be better by your example.

45. Respect is a currency that is earned by our choices. It cannot be bought, and is not a Birthright.

46. Energy is universal to everything in existence.

47. Race, nationality, social standing, sexual orientation, appearance, or ability have no bearing on your character, intelligence, or potential.

48. Modern medicine should encourage natural remedies whenever possible.

49. Forgiveness is an act of self-preservation. It does not free others from guilt or responsibility, it merely frees you of the negative feelings.

50. Human interaction is a necessary part of well-being. Disassociation and withdrawal from contact harm our wellness as individuals.

If this list can help to build a common ground for mankind, then instantly our voices and intentions as nations of people will intensify. Making it difficult for governments or rulers to carry on unwise or careless acts. Having a unified voice can help to make our best health and well-being a priority. Having a common ground will create a fundamental understanding of one another. It will make it more difficult, morally, for those who intend to inflict pain on others. It will make it difficult for a person to hold tightly to prejudices against people that you have come to understand share the same ideals as you. It would make it difficult for the blatant pollution of waterways and natural areas as being allowable or acceptable. It can give those without faith a reason to do good by each other, and it can give those with faith more conviction. It will open the door to a new avenue of education and awareness for humanity. It would act as a global subconscious from which we make our choices by as individuals. Establishing an intellectual unity can have profound benefits in every corner of our activities as a civilization.

Countless people throughout history have dreamt of and theorized about unity of any kind. This age of technology and interconnectivity is the first time where we have the ability to actually manifest that unity. Ironically, it seems that we need it more than ever right now. This intellectual framework is the missing link in our story. Inevitably, it will start a new chapter for mankind, where we can have a common focus and goal. A new age where the popular trend is to treat each other respectfully in order to enjoy the best experience possible. An era where people are conscious of the impact of their choices, and are actively trying to create a more fulfilling society for their children and grandchildren.

PERCEPTION

As we've discussed, your perception is everything. The way that you see the experience of each moment determines the value it holds for you. I think of perspective in layers. Initially, in your average day you are aware of your job, goals, relationships, bills, responsibilities, likes, and dislikes. But this is a small portion of what your mind is perceiving as a whole. The difference between your subconscious and conscious minds, is determined by your own perception of your reality.

Aside from the events of your daily life, your mind is also managing and balancing the multitude of functions in your body. Constantly analyzing the requirements and needs in order to sustain. Your mind knows when a certain gland or organ is in need of a particular protein or amino acid, and recalls receiving it when you ate a certain food. A craving is then sent to your conscious mind "Ooh! I want roast beef!" Or "I need a glass of orange juice." When you make yourself aware of that function in your mind, your intuition toward your health strengthens. If you listen when your body whispers you'll never have to hear it scream.

Your mind is also monitoring your location and movement. It is keeping track of which direction you travel, and where your home is at all times. It is aware of where you are geographically in correlation to the magnetic fields around you. It is aware that you are on a planet that is spinning about 1,000 miles per hour, and which direction that is. It is as well aware of your current position in our galaxy, and where we are in relation to the sun. Making yourself aware of that aspect of your mind broadens your perception of reality.

Your mind is as well aware of your entire genetic family history. Your DNA carries a history of the trials and tribulations of your ancestors. It's in every cell of your body. As your physical and mental needs change, and the environment around us changes, your mind adapts your ability to the environment and situations that you're in. Always learning new skills or thought processes to meet the need of your life. Permanent changes to your DNA coding take place through your life as your adaptations prove themselves to be productive. Making yourself aware of the evolution that you are experiencing gives profound purpose to most obstacles, challenges, victories, and lessons.

Your mind is also constantly aware of energy in many forms. It is aware of the amount of energy that is stored in your body. How much you will likely exert in that day. The constant waves of radiation and light coming from the Sun, as well as the infrared light that passes right through us. Energy is in every morsel of our body, and everything that exists around us. Including that exchange in your perception makes this experience amazing!

On a whole other level, your mind is monitoring your intuitions for things. It feels when someone is looking at you, and what their intention is. It feels when someone is thinking about you, or talking about you. It feels when someone you love is in need. It feels the inadvertent thoughts of those who are in your daily life, and their opinions of you. As well as any other entities that may be in your perception. It monitors the intentions of every single person you pass by. Mainly in the effort of defense or self-preservation. Your mind has to make an opinion of what it thinks everyone is up to. It has intuitions of possible outcomes and future situations. Literally looking into the past and future on different possible pathways before making certain choices. Keeping this perspective in mind takes the walls down of your perception of reality.

Somewhere above all of that other activity, your mind upholds a sense of well being. How you feel about everything it is that you feel. Overseeing the big picture and conjuring your passions. This overall view is your higher self. The eternal part of you. The portion of your consciousness that is the narrator of all that is transpiring in your story. The part of you that scolds your conscious mind when you are out of line, or creating some kind of long-term struggle with a certain choice. This part of your consciousness will step in the way of your normal daily activities if something is amiss. Often you won't be able to put your finger on why you feel a certain way suddenly, but you don't get to discredit it. Often times, when you do ignore this higher intuition towards things you end up regretting it for what transpired afterward. Knowing that you "should've listened to yourself". This part of your consciousness is not impressed with superficial pleasures or ambitions. It's the part of your mind that knows your destiny and tries to keep you on track. Keeping this level of consciousness and awareness throughout your day makes maneuvering through your choices effortless. You know automatically what the right and wrong answers are to every choice you face in your day.

It can be difficult to wrap your head around all that's going on in your head. But with some practice, your perception itself can expand to encompass all that your mind is actually processing. Because of our short attention span, our conscious mind is not allowed to be in control of things like our bodily functions, hand/eye coordination, or sense of gravity. But the experience of life becomes far more intricate and jaw dropping when you bear into consideration how much interaction you are actually doing in each mundane moment.

An enlightened perspective…

Everything is energy. From as far out in space as I can imagine, to each microscopic particle of who I am. All of my thoughts and actions are a matter of my energy being amazingly orchestrated by my mind in order to carry out the intentions of my soul. Throughout the course of my day I only have so much energy that I can focus towards things. Which makes it important for me to choose to spend that energy wisely. I understand that I am able to choose the perspective that I view any situation with, so I am careful to not let my mind linger on unproductive thoughts. The main focus of each day is to try and enjoy the circumstances that I face to the best of my ability. In doing this not only do I feel better about myself, but I become an example to those around me who share the same circumstances. I understand that it's easy for me to be swayed by influences around me, so I try and selectively choose the influences I put in front of myself. If I look for negativity, I will find it. If I look for positivity I will find it. I am proactively trying to spread the influence that I would like to receive. I see that people are sometimes influenced by my actions, so I am proactive in trying to make the most positive impact on people that I can. I know that the positivity that I spread to people is reciprocated, and becomes waves of intention that will inevitably have spread throughout my city and back to me by nightfall.

I appreciate all that my life has held thus far. Which includes my mistakes and victories, my pains and cures, my good deeds and wrongs that I have caused, my ignorance and the epiphanies they have brought me to. All that I have been, experienced, and endured has brought me to the person that I am today. Each step in my story was necessary for me to reach this upgraded version of who I once was. My effort in each day is to make good by the intention that my past self and future self had for me on this day. If I can intellectually embrace my entire life and do right by my goals and an intentions, then I deserve my own pride and respect. The confidence that I carry for who I am creates a self satisfaction that cannot be harmed by outside influences.

When I am faced with angry or combative people, I understand that it is caused by frustration and insecurity, and I forgive their actions. As I enter situations, I carry an intention of what I would like to manifest, but no expectation of what the result will be. As I walk away from situations I accept them as having unfolded the way that they were supposed to, and I remain confident in the influence that I offered. I know that while people and circumstances are not in my control, my response to them is. Whatever situation or circumstance I find myself in I do my very best to take it gracefully, and communicate productively. I understand intimately how difficult and disheartening life can be, so I don't pass judgment on people that are troubled by it. I realize that while I can try and hide how I really feel about myself for things, it is still evident to the people around me.

I am aware of the incredible relationship of interdependence of life that exists within my body. I see that same relationship of interdependence in every being around me as well. More importantly, I see the incredible relationship of interdependence that I share with all that life around me. I realize that in a small way, I am affecting the success of every creature in my environment by my influence. From plant life to my family. From each cell of my body to the collective consciousness of mankind. I also understand that my thoughts and intentions are received in whatever direction I focus them. Even if I feel insignificant to others, I am part of a massive team effort that depends on me to be my best. In a sense, I am merely a cell that is part of a grand organism.

I try to align my thoughts with what my intentions or desires are. I align my intentions with the goals that I set for myself. I align my goals with the way that I want to feel or be in the future. This is a deliberate effort to make myself the most effective tool for my own destiny that I can be. While I keep myself available for the people in my life, the main objective must always be my own joy or contentment. Everyone is depending on me, so if I let myself fall for the sake of one, I am not doing justice to the others, nor myself. In a beautifully ironic way, my self preservation is the best way that I can serve my team.

I know that change is the only constant in the universe. This being the case, I try not to allow myself to get too attached to any particular circumstance. My condition is not my conclusion. I try to keep myself ready and expecting of change, and I take it as a challenge, and not a sentence. I am the recipient of the unique set of circumstances that has brought me to this day, not the victim of them. I know that although I'm smart enough to conjure excuses and justifications for why I don't do my best, the energy is better spent actually trying to do my best. I make effort to keep my responsibilities handled and relationships strong, because I know that things can change in an instant. Absolutely nothing is guaranteed in this world, and I am thankful for all that I have. Being prepared mentally for each possible outcome ensures my successful handling of things in the future, and soothes any fears I may have.

I take each day as a new opportunity. A chance for me to achieve things that were previously out of my reach. A chance to get one step closer to reaching my goals. A chance to exceed my ancestors expectations of what I could be. A chance to connect with a stranger or loved one in a profound way that affects us both for the rest of our days. An opportunity to find even a moment of bliss or spiritual ecstasy amongst the random exchange of existence. Each day is a chance for me to understand more fully, or even perhaps master a feeling of peace and enlightenment. Each day is an opportunity for me to expand the ability of my intentions and intuitions. Each day is a chance for me to be an example to someone who needs it. Each day is an opportunity for me to end that day with a smile and feeling of contentment as I fall asleep. Each day is a profound gift that I am not promised. My life may come to an end at any particular point, so I carry a reverence for being able to participate just one more time. A chance for me to fully grasp the Incredible and amazing experience of this ironic and romantic global interconnected relationship we all share on the path to our destinies. I allow myself to be in complete awe of the higher power and magnificent orchestration of fate and karma around me.

My soul is a conglomeration of energy encoded with the history of my existence. It has an intention of it's own for my life and choices. It has the objective of making life-long friends, experiencing as much as possible, and making choices that facilitate a progression of that energy. It is on it's way to a feeling called enlightenment, where a universal acceptance filters my dispositions toward everything. It is what fuels my ambitions, intuitions, and dreams for my future. It is what will leave my body when I die. When I'm gone others will be left with my memory and the impact I've made on their souls. My specific frequency of energy is the way that other souls recognize my intentions and spirit in this life, or afterward. My soul is the reason my body lives, and the purpose behind this journey called life. I am mindful of that fact, and give respect to the possibility of centuries of cumulative karma that may have led up to this day. I am more than my name, birthday, race, religion, family, responsibilities, and legacy. I am (in one form or another) eternal. As well are you…

There are many different paths to a feeling of enlightenment. Most of which are through religious practice and surrendering to a power greater than yourself. Some even find a sense of enlightenment through a scientific perspective as well. Explore your own spirit and mind and find a method that makes sense to you. You must believe whole-heartedly in whichever path you choose, as your own conviction to that path of growth decides your success.

While you may not share my perspective, you can likely appreciate it. It suits my heart, mind, and soul. I'm able to maneuver through my days without carrying uncomfortable baggage. I am able to have a deep appreciation and admiration of all of the life around me. I love everyone, regardless of who they are or what they've done. I see beings as miracles living their lives, doing miraculous things, on an epic and miraculous journey to enlightenment, that spans throughout history. This, my dear friends, is jaw dropping life in High-Definition! I welcome you to see the view from here!

ABOUT THE AUTHOR

This book indirectly references many different sources. This includes every leading religious way of belief on the planet, every leading quantum theory that's widely accepted, numerous documented research studies, and the general opinions of a multitude of different people. This book indirectly references the wisdom of many different authors, philosophers, and influential people throughout history. This book is an accumulation of the lives and perspectives of thousands of different people. In a sense, credit is due to everyone who has actively participated in the history of mankind. Each different perspective is an important and even necessary piece of the cumulative wisdom that we all share.

We share the same condition, curriculum, society, struggles, and need for understanding and peace. We all have a good idea of the difference between right and wrong, and dance somewhere between the two. We all wish for a better moral and social standard for us to call "normal," because this is the standard that we judge ourselves by and use to justify our shortcomings as individuals and citizens. We want to treat each other respectfully and be a decent person, but it's uncomfortable to be the only one doing so. A basic intellectual or spiritual common ground will create a new sense of normality. It will raise the standard that which we live by, socially. This book and movement is very much a group effort, and will require each of our perspectives to fully represent mankind.

This book is not about the perspectives of all of those who helped create it, this book is about YOU, has been created for YOU, and is written by YOU. Any recognition that this book may receive will be shared by all of YOU... Team Human.

www.ingramcontent.com/pod-product-compliance
Lightning Source LLC
LaVergne TN
LVHW040159080526
838202LV00042B/3227